To; FRANK
HAVE FUN WITH MY BOOK

GREAT UNCLE
Theo. F. Buntillo
1/1/00

TED PUNTILLO

THE TOADS OF DAVIS

A SAGA OF A SMALL TOWN

Dedication

This book is dedicated to the memory of my wife Mary Grindell Puntillo and to my beautiful granddaughters, Sadie, Sara and April.

I would also like to acknowledge my family and friends
who have supported and encouraged me,
including my sons, Ted and Ed,
Mel Gagnon, Jim and Fran Schmerbauch,
Gail Catlin and Lisa Bacchini.

The Toads of Davis
A Saga of a Small Town

For more information, or to order additional copies:

T.P. Products
P.O. Box 4444
Davis, CA 95617
Phone/Fax: (530) 757-1935
Website: toadsofdavis.com

Puntillo, Ted
The Toads of Davis—A Saga of a Small Town/Ted Puntillo
p. cm.
Summary: The toads of Davis escape disaster with the help of city officials and the community.

ISBN: 0-9674417-0-6
Library of Congress Number:

All text and illustrations the original work of Ted Puntillo
Edited by Gail Catlin
Cover design and text layout by Lisa Bacchini Graphic Design and Illustration
Back cover photo: Donna Carrigg

10 9 8 7 6 5 4 3 2 1

Printed in Korea
First printing, October 1999

The illustrations in this book are done with acrylic paint on watercolor paper.

This is the story

of a
happy
community
of toads.

They lived in a pond on the
outskirts of a California town
named

Davis.

The Davis toads had lived peacefully
for many years in their little town.
The people of the town
had always enjoyed the toads,
and had been very considerate
not to harm the toads' field and pond.

During the day, the Davis toads
did what most ordinary toads do.

They swam, they slept
under their favorite tree,
and they talked with their friends
about what was happening
in their toad neighborhood.

They also imitated the people of Davis by playing sports…
in a toad sort of way.

The toads loved to play golf, tennis and especially toad softball.

Leap-frogging also was a favorite pastime.

The toads shouted
"Whee! You can't catch me,"
as they hopped
over one another.

Teaching their young about their great history was another daily toad activity.

The elder toads taught the youngsters the difference between toads, which spend most of their time on land, and frogs, which mainly prefer water.

The toads also
liked to read
and play music.

Toads are
good at
having fun.

When the
toads were
hungry
they were very fond
of toad pizza.

They knew
they could always
call Hoppy's Pizza,
and have a
nice bug pizza
delivered
to tide
them over.

During the winter
the toads were content
to stay in their
cold weather habitat.

The pond
was always
full of water
and the
cool temperature
made them
very happy.

Ｂut the highlight of the year
was the annual
Spring Toad Migration
across the grassy plain
to the cozy ivy
growing beside the
Davis Post Office.

DAVIS
POST OFFICE

When the toads arrived after their long
journey, the friendly Davis postal workers
would feed them, and enjoy their company
as the toads jumped and played.

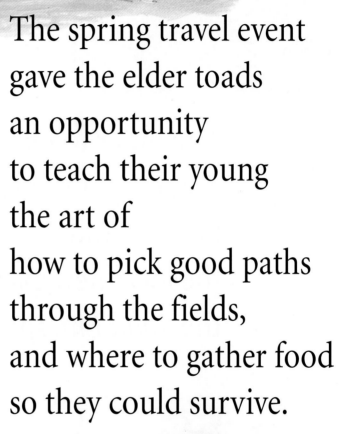

The spring travel event
gave the elder toads
an opportunity
to teach their young
the art of
how to pick good paths
through the fields,
and where to gather food
so they could survive.

The older toads
also taught the younger ones
how to read
the local newspaper,
the *Toad Enterprise.*

One day when
the *Toad Enterprise*
arrived,
it had an article
that was interesting
and scary.

The city of Davis was planning
to build a new automobile road
with a big overpass
that would cut right through
the toads' migration trail!

The toads were concerned.
Now they would have to
out-hop the speeding cars
to get to the post office!

A toad town meeting was called.
"We need to discuss what to do!"
the toad elders said.
"We must let the
people of Davis
know what
this overpass
will do to us,"
one toad
croaked out.

TOADARY CLUB

The toads went straight
to the Davis townspeople
to let them know how much
this new road
would affect their village life.

"Please let the
city council know
how we feel,"
they begged.

The toads
were very upset.

Some cried
big toad tears.

The toads
even helped the citizens
by making signs.

The people of Davis
responded with
an outpouring of support.

They marched, carried posters
and put their names
on petitions.
"Save our Toads!"
was the unhappy cry
from the upset citizens.

They even showed their support
by placing big signs
on the famous tunnel
into downtown Davis,
telling everyone about
the big problem.

The city council
discussed the toads' problem
for months.

Finally the mayor said,
"We must save our friendly amphibians."
The whole city council agreed.

They decided to build a toad tunnel
under the new overpass,
so the toads could still migrate
to the shady post office in the spring,
without fear of being run over
by cars.

The toads were very happy
with the city council's decision
to do something for them.
They croaked with joy.

Building started
on the overpass.
The curious toads
watched as
workers pounded stakes
and put up
large wooden timbers.

Tractors roared,
and huge amounts of dirt
were moved to
build the overpass.
    The toads were amazed
    at the power
    of the big machines.

Large trucks
poured cement
day after day.
    The earth shook every time
    a truck dumped its load.
    The toads wondered
    if all the construction
    would ever end.

The postal workers were very careful
not to endanger the toads.
They always yielded
to the toads' right-of-way.
A toad crossing guard
was set up to protect
the little toads
who might wander near the street.

Finally,
the workers started digging
the toad tunnel.
It started at the
toad pond
and ended up
at the post office.

Everyone was talking about the tunnel.

The topic at the local barbershop, and on every street corner was the toad tunnel.

One day,
the postmaster
at the Davis Post Office
was talking with his father
about the toads
and the tunnel.

TITANIC TED   POSTMASTER

TOAD HOLLOW

They thought
that the toads
might become tired
after hopping so long
on the new tunnel journey.

Aha!! A solution:
Build a little toad resting place
at the end of the tunnel
…a toad resort!

The postmaster's father
went right to work.
He built a toad-sized motel,
cafe, juice bar, outhouse
and swimming pool.
> The juice bar was complete
> with toad stools to sit on,
> and served organic juice
> for thirsty toads.
> The resort was named "Toad Hollow."

The toads heard
of this idea
and were overjoyed
that someone
cared so much
about them.

They were
spreading the word
about the resort
with a
"canference" call.

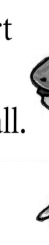

After many months
the overpass was complete…
and so was the toad tunnel
to Toad Hollow.
The Toads had
a "ribbit" cutting
to celebrate the opening
of the tunnel
and Toad Hollow.

The time had come
to make the first journey
through the toad tunnel.
Many toads prepared themselves
for the journey
by checking their flashlights
and lanterns.

Since there were
no lights in the
tunnel,
it was very dark.

The toads were also
building vehicles to help them
make their long journey.

A nice wooden box
and some old roller skates
made a fine scooter.

The toads packed
their belongings
for the trip.

The eldest toad
was given the honor
of being the first
to travel through the tunnel.

"Perfect! No problems,"
he yelled out.

W hen the toads arrived
at Toad Hollow,
their new resort,
the toads instantly
felt at home.

They began playing
and having fun,
doing all the toad things
they normally did.

The toads played
their musical
instruments
and sang
all night long.

The music
was loud,
but no one
complained.

The local barbershop quartet,
"The Mellow Toads," sang the
praises of all the concerned citizens
who helped them, and everyone danced
in their organic juice bar, "Toadwerks."

The toads toasted
the citizens of Davis
for caring so much about them.
They knew they were very lucky
to live in a town like Davis,
where people
really loved them.

They posted signs
in celebration.

One toad even
passed out balloons
to the children.

As word spread about what the people of Davis had done for the toads, television, radio and newspaper reporters came from all over the world to learn about the toad tunnel and Toad Hollow.

They interviewed everyone involved, including the postmaster's father who had built the resort.

They also talked to everyone else involved in the project to save the toads.

The story was in newspapers and on television stations all over the world.

The excitement was always the same:

Look what one small town did for nature!

Look at what a special place the city of Davis is!

Today,
the toads still love
their new tunnel and resort.
  They are happier than ever
  in their summer habitat
  by the post office.

Local schools tour Toad Hollow
to teach students how a town's action
and care can save wildlife and
share space with all of nature's creatures.
School children also learn how
communities can plan and build roads
and buildings in ways that preserve the
environment rather than harm it.

We must remember that this place we call Earth belongs to everyone, and we must care for every living creature that inhabits it.

ABOUT THIS BOOK

The Masai people of Africa are known to greet each other by asking, "How are the children?" It is this indigenous people's belief that the welfare of all the people can be gauged by the well-being of the smallest among them. Conversely, if the children are not well, then the community is also not well. This is an important perspective to consider as we enter the new millennium.

The Toads of Davis is a children's tale, but it is also a true story of a community that is willing to ask, "How are the smallest among us?" and to take action to assure the welfare of all. In this way, this community contemplates and assures its future. It is our hope that in telling the story of *The Toads of Davis* we can inspire other communities to consider the welfare of all living things.

To order additional copies of this book contact:
T.P. Products
P.O. Box 4444
Davis, CA 95617
Phone/Fax (530) 757-1935
Website: toadsofdavis.com

46